W9-BXM-607

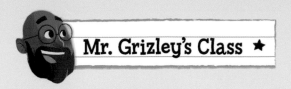

Mr. Grizley's Class ★

Nathan's

New Moves

by Bryan Patrick Avery   illustrated by Arief Putra

PICTURE WINDOW BOOKS
a capstone imprint

Published by Picture Window Books,
an imprint of Capstone.
1710 Roe Crest Drive
North Mankato, Minnesota 56003
capstonepub.com

Library of Congress Cataloging-in-Publication Data is
available on the Library of Congress website.

ISBN: 9781666339246 (hardcover)
ISBN: 9781666339253 (paperback)
ISBN: 9781666339260 (ebook PDF)

Summary: Nathan is planning to perform a comedy act for the
talent show. But when Chad needs a new hip-hop dance partner,
Nathan has to decide which act to do.

Designed by Dina Her

Printed and bound in the USA. PO4882

TABLE OF CONTENTS

Mr. Grizley's Class ★

Cecilia Gomez

Shaw Quinn

Emily Kim

Mordecai Foster

Nathan Wu

Ashok Aparnam

Ryan Clayborn

Rahma Abdi

Nicole Washington

Alijah Wilson

Suddha Agarwal

Chad Werner

Semira Madani

Pierre Boucher

Zoe Charmichael

Dmitry Orloff

Camila Jennings

Madison Tanaka

Annie Barberra

Bobby Lewis

CHAPTER 1

Late Start

Nathan waited outside of class with his classmates. Mr. Grizley was late.

"Hey, Nathan," Rahma said. "Do you have any new jokes?"

"Well," Nathan said, "I've been saving my new jokes for the talent show."

"Come on," Chad begged.
"Just one joke?"

"Okay, just one," Nathan
said. "Why didn't the ghost go
to the movies?"

Chad scratched his head.
"I don't know," he said.

"Because he had no *body* to go with!" Nathan grinned. His classmates laughed.

"You're so funny," Madison said.

"Yeah," Rahma agreed. "I bet you'll be the best today's talent show."

"Not so fast," Chad said.
"Alijah and I are doing our new
hip-hop dance."

Chad did a spin and jumped
up into the air. He landed doing
the splits.

"Hey!" Nathan laughed.
"I taught you that!"

Chad smiled. "Well, Alijah and I perfected it."

Nathan looked around. "Where is Alijah?" he asked.

Mr. Grizley rushed toward the class. "Sorry I'm late," he said. "Come inside. I have some bad news."

CHAPTER 2

Bad News

"Alijah was in an accident yesterday," Mr. Grizley announced.

The class gasped.

"He's going to be fine," Mr. Grizley continued. "But he has a fractured ankle."

"When can he come back to school?" Ashok asked.

"I'm not sure," Mr. Grizley said. "But Alijah is our friend. What do we say about friends?"

"We always support our friends!" the class answered.

"Right!" Mr. Grizley said. "Let's each make a card for Alijah. We can do it now, before we start our day. I'll take them over to him after our talent show."

The class got to work. Zoe handed out paper. Ryan passed out markers.

Nathan drew a huge happy face on his card. He wrote one of his funniest jokes on the inside.

Chad tapped Nathan on the shoulder.

"I need a favor," Chad said.
"Since Alijah can't do the talent
show, and you know all the
moves, will you do it with me?"

"I don't know," Nathan said. "That will mean I can't do my jokes."

"*Please?*" Chad begged. "It could be a tribute to Alijah."

"I'll think about it," Nathan said.

CHAPTER 3

Helping a Friend

Nathan didn't think about it for long. He finished his card and went to talk to Mr. Grizley.

"I won't be able to do my comedy act for the talent show," Nathan said. "I'm going to do a hip-hop dance with Chad instead."

Mr. Grizley smiled.

"You're going to take Alijah's place?" he asked.

"Yes," Nathan said. "Chad asked for my help."

At recess, Chad and Nathan practiced their dance.

They swayed and hopped and spun.

They took a break. Then they
did it all again.

By the end of recess, they
were ready.

At the talent show, Emily juggled soccer balls.

Dmitry played a flute while riding a unicycle.

Mordecai made Shaw
disappear.

It was quite a show!

Nathan and Chad took the stage. Their heads bobbed to the music. They spun and danced and swayed.

At the end, they each did a
backflip. When they landed with
their fists in the air, the class
cheered.

After the show, Mr. Grizley talked to Nathan.

"It was kind of you to dance with Chad," Mr. Grizley said.

"Well," Nathan said, "it wasn't a hard choice. I was just supporting my friend."

LET'S MAKE A GREETING CARD

Greeting cards are a wonderful way to say thank you, wish someone well, or let somebody know you're thinking about them. Mr. Grizley's class made greeting cards for Alijah when he was hurt in an accident. Let's make a greeting card to give to a friend, teacher, or relative.

WHAT YOU NEED:
- white or colored paper
- markers or crayons

WHAT YOU DO:
1. Choose who you want to give a card to and why. For example, Nathan created a card for Alijah to help him feel better.

2. Fold your paper in half. This will give your card an inside and an outside.

3. Decorate the outside of the card however you would like. Sometimes, it's nice to put something the person receiving the card would like. If you're giving the card to someone who likes unicorns, you could draw a unicorn on the front.

4. Inside the card, write a message to the person the card is for. It can be something short, like "Happy Birthday," or something longer, like a letter or a poem. Feel free to decorate the inside of the card too.

5. Make sure to sign your name so they know who the card is from.

That's it. Your greeting card is done. Make sure to deliver it. People love to get cards and letters. If you need to mail it, ask an adult for help.

GLOSSARY

accident (AK-suh-duhnt)—a sudden and unexpected event that leads to loss or injury

comedy act (KOM-i-dee AKT)—a performance act where someone tells jokes

fractured (FRAK-churd)—broken or cracked

funniest (FUHN-ee-ehst)—being the most funny

perfected (per-FEK-ted)—made perfect

scratch (SKRACH)—to scrape or rub lightly

support (suh-POHRT)—to help someone and encourage them to be their best

tribute (TRIB-yoot)—a performance given in honor of someone

TALK ABOUT IT

1. Mr. Grizley had to tell the class about Alijah's accident. Have you ever had to tell someone bad news? How did you do it? Was it easy or hard to do?

2. Besides making a card, what are some other things you could do to help someone feel better?

3. Why did Nathan need time to think before agreeing to dance with Chad in the talent show? Have you ever had to give up something you wanted to help someone else?

WRITE ABOUT IT

1. A program lists all the acts or songs in a show. Using details from the story, create a program for the class talent show.

2. Pretend you are in Mr. Grizley's class and make a card for Alijah. Be sure to write a special message to him.

3. This story is about supporting friends. Write a paragraph about a time a friend supported you.

ABOUT THE AUTHOR

Bryan Patrick Avery discovered his love of reading and writing at an early age when he received his first Bobbsey Twins mystery. He writes picture books, chapter books, middle grade, and graphic novels. He is the author of the picture book *The Freeman Field Photograph*, as well as "The Magic Day Mystery" in *Super Puzzletastic Mysteries*. Bryan lives in northern California with his family.

ABOUT THE ILLUSTRATOR

Arief Putra loves working and drawing in his home studio at the corner of Yogyakarta city in Indonesia. He enjoys coffee, cooking, space documentaries, and solving the Rubik's Cube. Living in a small house in a rural area with his wife and two sons, Arief has a big dream to spread positivity around the world through his art.